THE FOOTBALL TRIALS

KICK OFF

BLOOMSBURY EDUCATION
Bloomsbury Publishing Plc
50 Bedford Square, London, WC1B 3DP, UK

BLOOMSBURY, BLOOMSBURY EDUCATION and the Diana logo
are trademarks of Bloomsbury Publishing Plc

First published in Great Britain 2018 by Bloomsbury Publishing Plc

A catalogue record for this book is available from the British Library

ISBN: PB: 978-1-4729-4411-5; ePDF: 978-1-4729-4412-2; ePub: 978-1-4729-4409-2

2 4 6 8 10 9 7 5 3 1

Cover design by James Fraser Design
Typeset by Integra Software Services Pvt. Ltd.

Printed and bound in China by Leo Paper Products

To find out more about our authors and books visit
www.bloomsbury.com and sign up for our newsletters

recommended by

www.catchup.org

Catch Up is a charity which aims to address the problem of underachievement
that has its roots in literacy and numeracy difficulties.

THE FOOTBALL TRIALS
KICK OFF

JOHN HICKMAN
Illustrated by NEIL EVANS

BLOOMSBURY EDUCATION

LONDON   OXFORD   NEW YORK   NEW DELHI   SYDNEY

CONTENTS

The Scout

"Who is that old geezer watching us?" asks Wheeler.

I look to where Wheeler is pointing and I see an old man standing there, with a little dog. He has white hair and a fat Father Christmas belly.

"Come on, let's just play on," I say.

The four of us are having a kick about in the park. Wheeler, me, Taylor and Harj. Two on two. We've put our coats down to mark the goals. We come here most days after school to play football.

"RIGHT," I shout. "NEXT GOAL WINNER!"

Taylor comes at me with the ball, with his Arsenal shirt on. He's the only one who supports Arsenal. Muppet. The rest of us are United through and through. He tries to pop the ball through my legs.

"As if!" I say. I take the ball away from his feet and nutmeg him instead.

I want to try something different. The Rabona. I've seen it online.

Instead of just shooting with my right, like I normally do, I flick my right foot around the back of my left and hit the ball hard. I almost tie myself up in a knot doing it. The ball flies straight between the coats.

"LOVELY GOAL!" shouts the old man.

Wheeler grabs the ball and we all go over.

"Why are you watching us?" asks Wheeler.

"I wasn't watching you," says the old man. "I was watching him." He points at me.

"What... what you watching me for?" I ask.

"I'm a scout," says the old man.

"Bit old to be a scout aren't you?" says Wheeler. "And shouldn't you have lots of badges on your shirt?"

"I'm not that sort of scout," says the old man.

"I'm a football scout. For United." He pulls out a business card and hands it to me. It says "Arthur Logan: Football scout". There's a phone number and email address, and United's logo printed in the corner.

"I'm Arthur," he says. He holds out his hand.

I shake it. The others do the same.

"I heard there was a kid with some skill – a little rough around the edges – but a real player," he says.

"Who told you that?" I ask.

"A little bird," he says and taps his nose.

"You think Jax has got what it takes?" asks Harj.

"He's got something," says Arthur. "If you want a trial, I can make that happen for you. What was your name again?"

"Jackson," I tell him. "Jackson Law."

"If I were you, I'd sign him now. Fifty K a week," says Taylor.

Arthur laughs. "If you want that trial, give me a call," he says. He nods at me, then walks away with his little dog.

"You could play in the Premier League," says Wheeler. "How awesome is that?"

I take a breath. I feel a bit dizzy and sick. It's a joke. Has to be. But what if it isn't? Could I really get signed by United?

Man, this is PROPER crazy!

The Golden Ticket

I live in the flats not far from the park. I run up the stairs, because the lift breaks down all the time. When I get inside our flat, I kick off my trainers. Granddad already has his tea on his lap in the living room. Sausage and mash.

Granddad has thick grey hair and tattoos all over his arms. He's a big man. He used to do loads of weights, but he can't now. He's got an illness called MS. That stands for Multiple Sclerosis. Since they worked out what was wrong with him, he's just got worse and worse. He can't walk without a stick now. Mum thinks he'll be in a wheelchair this time next year.

That's why he lives with us. He stopped being able to do things around his own house. Had to give up driving his taxi too. I like having him around though. I just wish it wasn't because he had this horrible disease inside him.

Mum comes in holding my plate of sausage and mash. "Here you go," she says.

"Thanks." I shovel a forkful into my mouth.

Mum sits on the sofa next to me with her own plate. She's wearing her horrible Quickstop uniform. She works on the checkout there. I wish she didn't have to work as much as she does. She can go on a bit sometimes, but she does her best for me and Granddad. And I know it's only because she cares.

"What are you grinning about?" asks Granddad.

I've been waiting to tell them. I'm proper excited. I take out the card and hand it to Mum. "Check this out," I say.

Mum frowns. "Who gave you this?" she asks.

"Some old guy," I tell her. "He said he could sort me out a trial at United."

"You're kidding me!" says Granddad. "I knew you had it, son. I knew it!"

"Don't fill his head with nonsense," says Mum. "It might be dodgy."

My heart sinks.

"Let's have a look," says Granddad.

Mum hands Granddad the card.

He takes his glasses from the little table next to him and puts them on. He holds the card away from him and squints at it. "Arthur Logan... hmmm, where do I know that name?" Then a smile breaks across his face. "He used to play for United. Back in the seventies. Centre half. Hard as nails he was. When is your trial?"

"Dunno," I tell him. "The man said I needed to ring up."

"Right, no problem," says Granddad. "Leave it with me."

"Don't get his hopes up," says Mum.

"Why not?" asks Granddad. "It's not every day you get offered a trial with United. Could be just what the lad needs."

"Or it could just be a disappointment," says Mum.

"You know what this reminds me of?" says Granddad. *Charlie and the Chocolate Factory.* And you my boy, have just found the golden ticket!"

"Shouldn't you be in bed with loads of other old people?" I ask.

"Chance would be a fine thing!" he says.

"Dad!" Mum says, laughing. "I'm trying to eat!"

***

Later that night, I sit and listen while Granddad is on the phone.

"This Saturday?" he says. Then he nods. "About ten? Brilliant, we'll see you there." He ends the call and grins at me. "Right then, all sorted. This Saturday at ten."

"This Saturday?" I ask, hoping he doesn't mean the day after tomorrow.

"This Saturday," he repeats. "Excited?"

"Yeah," I say, doing my best to grin back. And I am excited, of course I am. But I'm also scared. People talk about having butterflies in their tummy when they're excited and nervous. Whatever is in my belly feels like a swarm of angry bees, all big and fat, buzzing about, banging into each other.

"You'll be fine," says Granddad.

"Yeah," I say again, like it's the only word I know. I'm really not sure I'll be fine at all.

Second Thoughts

When the day of my trial comes around,
Granddad comes with me on the bus. I pay
the driver because Granddad's illness means
he finds it difficult to get coins out of his
pockets. We sit at the front of the bus.

Granddad groans in pain, even though he tries to hide it. Mum says he's always in pain. He doesn't complain though. It's rubbish that nice people like my granddad have to live in pain. I wish I could help – do something for him and for my Mum. I wish I could buy them a nice house away from here. If things with United work out, maybe I could...

I take a deep breath.

"You'll be OK," says Granddad. "Just have some belief in yourself."

"I'll try," I tell him.

"George Best was one of the best footballers I've ever seen," he says. "They said he was too small, you know. Too small. Can you believe that? If he had listened, he would never have made it.

"But he didn't give up. Self-belief and determination," he says. "That's what you need. And hard work. Discipline. Talent..."

"Not much then!" I say.

He laughs. "You've got the talent," he tells me. "You just need to work hard and believe in yourself."

* * *

As we get closer to Samuels Park – the place where United's academy and training ground are based – the little belief I have starts dribbling away. What am I doing? Me, play for United? As if.

What if I'm not as good as I think? What if the other kids there are better than me? They've probably been playing together since they were seven. Then there's me, coming in at fifteen. They won't pass to me. They'll probably just think I'm some tramp from some scummy estate.

By the time the bus arrives at the stop, I've got no belief at all. All I've got is fear. I help Granddad off the bus and we walk slowly up to the big metal gates. Through them I can see huge white buildings with giant glass windows.

"I can't do this," I say.

"'Course you can," says Granddad.

"No, Granddad, I really can't."

I walk away.

"JACKSON!" Granddad shouts at me. "JACKSON! COME BACK!"

No Regrets

I can still hear Granddad shouting as I walk away. I feel horrible for leaving him.

"Jackson?" I hear someone call my name.

There's a car driving along slowly on the road next to me.

I look through the opened window.

Arthur, the scout, stares at me. "Where you going?" he asks.

"I'm... I'm, erm..."

"JACKSON!" Granddad shouts again.

"No need to worry," says Arthur. "If it doesn't work out, it doesn't work out. No harm done."

Maybe he's right. And I know I would regret it if I gave up without even trying. Whenever I watched a match or had a kick about with my mates, I would think about it.

I take a breath, open the passenger door and help Granddad into the car. I tell him I'm sorry for ditching him, and Arthur drives us into the car park.

I climb out the car and go around to the back door. I help Granddad get out of the car.

"You're not going to run off and leave me again, are you?" he asks.

I shake my head. "I'm sorry."

"So you should be!" he says. Then he winks at me.

Arthur shows us in through a set of automatic glass doors and into a foyer. A man in a training top with DP on his chest is waiting there. "Darren," says Arthur, "This is Jackson."

Darren holds his hand out. "Nice to meet you," he says.

I shake his hand.

"And this is Jackson's granddad," says Arthur. "Can I leave them with you?"

"Yeah, no worries," says Darren. "I'll give them a quick tour and then we can get Jackson out on the pitch."

I nod. Then I take a breath.

Darren smiles at me. "It'll be fine. Nothing to worry about."

***

Samuels Park is amazing. Darren tells me they have ten pitches, where every level of player trains.

"Every United player trains here?" I ask.

"That's right," says Darren. "You'll see one or two first-teamers knocking about. I heard Souza has been in for some treatment on his thigh."

Javier Souza is one of my favourite players. He plays central midfield, which is where I like to play. He's hard as nails, as Granddad would say. I think about asking Darren whether I could get Souza's autograph, but I stop myself. I don't want to come across as some tourist on a day-trip.

Everything is state of the art. There are physiotherapy and massage rooms, gyms, 3G pitches, a sauna, classrooms and a TV studio where they interview players. There's even a fancy restaurant.

Darren shows us into the changing rooms. The place shines like the kitchens and bathrooms you see in the adverts on TV for bleach. Once Darren has shown me the toilets and the way onto the pitches, he gives me a training kit and tells me they'll see me outside.

"Good luck," says Granddad. He gives me a wink, then leaves.

I sit on the bench. There are designer clothes and expensive trainers all over the place. Just lying around. Thousands of pounds' worth of gear. I take a few deep breaths to try to calm myself.

I change into the training kit. The T-shirt is plain black with a blue stripe around the middle. On the chest there's the club badge.

I stare at myself in the mirror. I look the part. A United player.

I feel dizzy. I sit back down on the bench. I'm really not sure I can do this.

On Trial

Outside, there are loads of pitches. The grass is lush and green. I can see a bunch of lads gathered in a group on the nearest pitch. Darren is there too. Granddad is over by the touchline.

There must be about twenty lads. All sizes and colours. Some are huge. Some look like they could be at least twenty years old, even though it's the youth squad. A couple are smaller than some of the kids in year seven at school. They're all staring at me as I get closer.

"Jackson is it?" says a man, in shorts and a United hoodie. The initials LC are on his chest. He looks hard, someone you wouldn't mess with. "I'm Liam," he says. "Head coach of the under-sixteens."

I shake his hand.

"You've met Darren, my assistant," he says. "I won't introduce all the lads now. You won't remember their names. But introduce yourself, fellas," he says to the other players. "And be nice."

One of the lads is big, with a shaved head. Looks like he could bench-press me. He gives me a cold look then he stares at Granddad.

I hate it when people stare at Granddad. Or when they tut because he's slowing them down in the street or something. This MS thing that Granddad has got, it could happen to anyone. People should remember that.

"Right then, boys," says Liam. "We'll have a little kick around. Half a pitch. Darren, sort them into two teams."

Darren hands out bibs to every other player.

I get a bib. I see that the boy with the shaved head doesn't get one, so he'll be on the other team. Then another lad with a bib comes over.

"I'm Ollie," he says. He has blonde, boy-band hair and the whitest teeth I've ever seen.

"Jackson," I tell him.

The match kicks off.

The lads at the back play it about a bit. Then one knocks it over to me.

I try and take it with my instep, but my touch is off and the ball goes out of play.

I hear the boy with the shaved head say "Rubbish."

I take a breath. I need to relax. Focus.

My next touch is much better. I take the ball and lay it off to a teammate.

I run forward and get the ball again. Play a one-two. I feel good, confident. I chip the ball out to the right and the winger swings one in.

Shaved head leaps up, heads it clear.

I take the ball on my chest, thirty yards out.

Shaved head charges at me like a rhino.

I do a pirouette and take him out of the game completely. He doesn't know what day it is. I pretend to shoot with my right, but pull it onto my left. I belt it right into the top corner of the net. The other lads look over and nod. I get a few pats on the back.

"GOOD GOAL," shouts Granddad.

"Who is that old freak?" asks shaved head, pointing at Granddad.

"What did you just say?" I ask. I can feel my anger rising.

"Who's that old freak?" he asks again.

I lose it. I shove him in the chest.

He comes back and pushes me – hard.

That's it; I don't care how big he is.

But before I can get a dig in, Darren has his arms wrapped around me.

"TAKE HIM INSIDE," yells Liam.

Bad Attitude

"You need to calm down," says Granddad on the bus back home.

"Not you as well," I say. "I've had enough of that from that Liam."

Granddad takes a shifty look about the bus, then he leans over.

"Don't tell your mum I said this, but I was quite proud seeing you stand up to that lump of a lad."

I smile. "Whatever. It was never going to work out," I say.

"Why would you say that?" asks Granddad.

"I didn't really fit in," I say.

"You fit in wherever you want," he tells me.

"Too late now anyway. I've blown it," I say sadly.

"You don't know that," he says.

"Think I do," I say.

***

That night, I have a kick about with Wheeler and the lads. When I get home, I'm surprised to find Liam in the living room talking with Mum and Granddad.

"All right, sweetheart," says Mum. "Liam has popped around to have a chat with us all." Mum has got a big smile on her face. Granddad is grinning. Even Liam is smiling too. I'm a bit freaked out.

"Good to see you again," says Liam.

"Is it?" I ask.

He laughs and shakes his head. "I was just telling your mum and granddad how talented you are."

"Really?" I ask.

"Yes, he was," says Mum.

"You're a little rough around the edges," says Liam. "But I want to give you a chance. See if we can polish you up a bit."

"You hear that?" says Granddad. "A diamond in the rough!"

"We've got a game coming up against Liverpool's under-sixteens," says Liam. "Wouldn't mind giving you a proper run out."

"Liverpool," says Mum. "They're good, aren't they?"

"Some good players in their academy," says Liam. "It'll be a test. You up for it?"

The under-sixteens? This is big. I don't care that those bumble bees are buzzing about in my belly again; I'm buzzing myself. "Yeah," I tell him. "I'm up for it."

Granddad winks at me. "Told you you would be OK," he whispers.

New Friends

That Friday, I step out on to the training
pitch. It still feels weird being here, at United.
It's like it's not quite real, like some movie,
or a video game or something, and I'm the
main guy.

Liam gathers us in a group. "OK, boys," he says. "Big game tomorrow, so nothing too heavy today. I want us to work on our short passing."

He sorts us out into two teams. I want to be on Ollie's team, but I'm not. Instead I get put with shaved head. Great.

We kick off a game of two touch. I only need two touches: one to control, one to put the ball wherever I want. I get a good feel for things. Score a couple of nice goals.

Shaved head, or Ryan as he's called, screams at me for the ball. He can scream. I lay it off to Zeki, another lad. Ryan won't get the ball from me. I just want to keep my head down. Play football. And ignore Ryan.

Liam blows the whistle. He gives us a few pointers about the match tomorrow, then he sends us away.

In the changing rooms, Ollie comes over.

"Well played," he says. "You've got some skill."

"Thanks, man," I tell him. "Pretty good yourself."

"What you pair of nerds talking about?" asks Ryan.

Neither of us says anything.

"About the other day," says Ryan. "I'm sorry about that."

This is a surprise. I'm not sure how to react, so I just tell him to forget about it.

"Pass me your phone," says Ryan.

"What for?" I ask.

"I'll give you my number," he says. "Text me. We could hang out together."

I'm a bit surprised, but I hand my phone to Ryan.

Ten minutes later, as I walk past Liam's office, Liam shouts at me: "Jackson, here a minute."

I step into his office. "Yeah?"

"Sit down," he tells me.

So I sit down.

"Do you want to tell me what you're playing at?" he asks.

I stare at him, confused.

He holds out his phone.

I'm even more confused.

"Don't play dumb," says Liam. "I've seen what you've posted."

I pull my phone out, and check my last post. It says, "Friday night = drink and drugs."

I stare at the words, unsure how they got there. Then it clicks. Ryan. I bet he posted it when he took my phone. My jaw goes tight.

"Well?" asks Liam. "What's going on?"

I think about telling the truth. I don't even drink. But what's the point? He wouldn't believe me. And anyway, I'm not a grass.

"I don't know," I say and I can hear how pathetic I sound. "Just a joke."

"Well it's not funny. When you play for this club, we expect certain standards," says Liam. "Do you understand? I took a chance bringing in a lad as old as you. I can't keep having these conversations with you," he says.

"Fine," I tell him. "You don't have to." Then I storm out.

Real Potential

Later that day, there's a knock on my bedroom door. Ollie from football comes in. "Alright, mate," he says. "Hope you don't mind me coming over. Got your address from Liam."

I scratch my neck, surprised to see him.

I wonder what kind of house Ollie lives in and feel myself go red with embarrassment.

"I didn't know what Ryan was up to," he says. "I only found out after. If I had known, I would have said something."

"Not your fault," I say.

"He can be such an idiot," he tells me. "He used to give me a hard time when I first started."

"You?" I ask.

"Yep. He thought I got special treatment," says Ollie.

"Why?" I ask.

"Doesn't matter," he says. "But Ryan is OK. Once you get to know him. He would do anything for a team-mate."

"Doesn't seem all that OK to me," I say.

"So is that it?" he asks. "Are you not coming back?"

I shake my head. "What's the point?"

"You should," he says. "You're a good player. That's why Ryan was giving you such a hard time. He can't stand anyone who is better than him."

I nod. That makes sense.

"Fancy coming over to my place to hang out sometime?" asks Ollie.

I nod my head.

"See you soon then," says Ollie as he turns to go.

***

A couple of days later, I head over to Ollie's house. He lives a bus ride away in Winter Hill, where all the footballers and local celebrities live. The houses are huge. More like mansions. And then I remember Ollie sitting in my tiny bedroom in the flat. I can't help but feel embarrassed.

I stop at the end of Ollie's huge driveway. There are big iron gates, just like the ones at the entrance to Samuels Park. Once I'm through the gates, there are trees all the way along a huge drive. I still can't believe Ollie lives in a place like this. I have no idea what his parents do but, whatever it is, they must get paid a tonne of money. Eventually I get to the house.

I ring the doorbell.

DINGGGG. DONGGGG.

Even the doorbell is epic.

Ollie answers. Inside the house, the hallway is massive. All marble and shiny, like a hotel or something. I reckon you could fit my whole flat in here.

There's this huge fish tank with all these bright tropical fish. I'd love to have a fish tank like that and I'm not even interested in fish!

Ollie's room is cool. There's the biggest TV I have ever seen and every console going. His shelf is filled with games. I look through them, seeing what he's got. It's like I'm in a shop. "What do your parents do?" I ask him. "Is your dad like a film star or something?"

"His dad is the manager of the world's greatest football team," says someone else.

My jaw drops.

Standing in the bedroom doorway, is Alex Chambers, the manager of United. "Do I look OK?" he asks, straightening his tie.

"You look fine, Dad," says Ollie.

Ollie's dad is Alex Chambers. Wow.

Alex Chambers is one of my all time heroes – one of the best managers in world football. They reckon he'll be England manager one day. We might actually have a chance of winning something with him in charge. Even Mum loves him and she hates football.

"So who is this?" asks Chambers.

"I'm Jackson," I tell him.

"Jackson Law?" he asks. "Liam has mentioned you. He tells me you've got a lovely left foot. He did also say you need to work on your attitude. Sort that out and you might have a chance." He winks at me. "I won't be back late," he says to Ollie. Then he ruffles Ollie's hair and goes down the stairs.

I stare at Ollie and blink a few times. "You never... why did you never..."

"I don't like to talk about it," he says. "Most people think I'm only in the team because of who my dad is."

Alex Chambers' words are like magic to me. A magic kick up the backside. If I'm ever going to get this, I need to learn to cope with being scared of failing. Messing up. I've got to get on with it. And I can't let other people stop me.

Apologies

The next day, I'm sitting in Liam's office again, with my tail between my legs. The door opens and Liam comes in. "Afternoon," he says.

"Thanks for seeing me," I say quietly.

He takes a seat behind his desk.

"Go on then, say what you need to say."

"I'm sorry," I tell him. "For walking out. For being an idiot."

"OK," he says.

"I really want to play for United," I tell him. "But even admitting that is hard. Because if I admit it, and I don't get it, I'll be proper gutted."

Liam nods.

"But I have to admit it, don't I?" I say. "Because I have to give it everything. If I hold back anything, I won't get it."

"OK, Jax," he says. "Apology accepted. But if we're going to move forward from here, I need to know I can trust you. Your bursts of bad temper can't go on. They are bad for you and bad for the club. Do you understand what I'm saying?"

"I understand," I tell him.

"Tell me what happened the other day,"
he asks.

I think about Ryan, how he stitched me up.
"I was just being stupid," I say.

"This job requires a lot," he says. "But above
all, it's about putting the team – the club – before
yourself. You're not going to always like your
team-mates, but you have to play with them."

"I know," I say.

"Good," says Liam. "There's a game on
Sunday against Chelsea's academy. If you
really want this, you'll need to be dedicated,
motivated..."

"I know," I say. "My granddad has been
through it all with me."

"No excuses then," he says.

"No excuses," I repeat. "I need to keep my
head together."

He nods and holds his hand out.

I shake it. Then I get up to leave.

"Oh and Jackson," says Liam.

I turn back.

"Thanks for coming to see me," he says. "You're a good lad."

I give him a nod and leave.

As I walk out of the gates, I feel good. I'm not going to let anything stand in my way.

The Big Match

Liam might have forgiven me, but I need to earn my place in the team. I stand at the side of the pitch and watch Chelsea batter us. 3–1 down at half-time.

All I want is to get out there, show everyone what I can do and help the team.

Liam gathers the lads together. "What's going on out there?" he asks.

"They're too quick," says Ryan.

"They're not," says Liam. "They just want it more. Look lads, do you want to play for United?"

Everyone nods.

"Because if you don't," says Liam, "there are plenty out there who do. So, I'll ask again, do you want to play for United?"

We all say "yes" this time.

"Well you need to fight," says Liam. "United never give up. It's in our DNA. You know this, lads. We can still win. OK?"

I look around at the other players. There are determined looks on their faces.

"Jackson," says Liam. "Get your jacket off. You're coming on."

We're all lined up before Chelsea have even finished their half-time team-talk. I look over at the side of the pitch. I notice Alex Chambers alongside Liam now. The nerves kick in.

And the second half kicks off.

Ollie and I work the ball well in midfield, making space and keeping possession. As the half goes on, I feel more and more confident. Every pass I hit is on point. The ball goes wherever I want.

Ryan deals with the Chelsea forwards and we take control of the game.

I get the ball in midfield. I spin away from a Chelsea player and find myself a few yards of space.

I dribble forward, dodge a few tackles, lay the ball off to Ollie and run on.

Ollie flicks the ball over their centre-backs.

I take it on my chest. Before the ball hits the ground, I rifle it with my right.

The keeper gets a palm to it, but the shot is too hard. He can't keep it out.

GOAL!

3–2.

I grab the ball from the net. The lads try and grab me as I race back to the halfway line, but I push them away. There's work to do.

They kick off. I'm on their forward as soon as he gets the ball. I slide in, take the ball and clatter the player. I look to the ref, but he waves play on.

Ollie is making a run into their box.

I hit a long pass from the centre circle.

It bounces in front of Ollie. He puts his foot through it.

Top corner of the net. What a strike.

3–3.

I race over to Ollie and the others who are celebrating near the corner flag.

Ollie points at me and everyone hugs me now.

For the rest of the half, we batter them. Every time we get the ball, we look as though we're going to score. It's only a combination of the woodwork and their keeper that stops us scoring five. But there are only a couple of minutes left and the scores are still level.

Chelsea's Brazilian kid gets the ball just outside the box.

He takes a shot, which is charged down by Ryan and out for a corner.

Chelsea bring everyone forward looking for the winner.

I pick up a big lad on the edge of the box. He tries to push and shove me, but I shove him back.

The ball comes in.

Ryan leaps up, towering above everyone else and heads it clear.

It drops to me.

The break is on.

I race away with the ball. Look up.

Ryan is sprinting forward.

I pretend to go left. Go right. Pass the defender with ease.

I'm at the edge of the box.

The Chelsea players are racing back towards their goal.

"JACKSON!" screams Ryan.

I think about cracking it. Getting the glory.

Then I think about Alex Chambers, Mum and Granddad. The team, and what Liam said.

I slip the ball through the defender's legs.

All Ryan has to do is make contact.

And he does.

The ball almost tears a hole in the back of the Chelsea net.

We go crazy.

Ryan jumps on me.

The pair of us tumble to the ground. The rest of the lads pile on. I'm buzzing.

The ref blows his whistle. We win 4–3. I shake the Chelsea players' hands. They all tell me I played well.

Ryan throws his arm around me. "Played, man," he says. He ruffles my hair and races over to his parents.

As I walk off the pitch, Liam calls me over. He's standing there with Alex Chambers. "That's what I've been talking about," says Liam. "This is what you can do. Do you see?"

"Got my eye on you," says Alex Chambers. He nods at me, then goes over to Ollie and puts his arm around him.

Ollie looks over at me and grins.

I grin back.

"Jackson," says someone else. It's Arthur, the scout. He's with my granddad. "Well played," he says. "You made your granddad proud."

"Thanks, Arthur," I tell him. "For everything."

"Thank **you**," he says. "You've made me look good." He tips his cap to me, then to my granddad and wanders off.

"Lovely fella," says Granddad.

I squint at him. "It was you, wasn't it?" I ask. "You told him about me."

"I'm saying nothing," says Granddad. He winks at me.

A New Team

A couple of weeks later, me and Wheeler are
having a kick about in the park. It's mad.
Seems like such a long time ago when Arthur
was watching me, but it's only been a month.

"BOYS!" shouts someone.

Ryan and Ollie are walking towards us.

I've started hanging out with Ryan and Ollie. Ollie is cool. Top boy. You know, he lives in this mansion and has everything anyone could ever want but he's the most down-to-earth person I've ever met. Ryan has started to grow on me too. He seems loyal: like a big, shaven-headed guard dog.

Things are going great at United. I've started the last two games and I feel like a proper part of the team. Liam says I've got a real chance of making it as a professional footballer, as long as I work hard and keep out of bother. I'm working hard. But keeping out of bother? I'll do my best!

"Safe, boys," I say.

Me and Wheeler bump fists with Ryan and Ollie.

"Give us a kick then," says Ryan.

I knock the ball to him.

He starts doing kick ups.

"All right, show off," says Wheeler. "Less of the fancy stuff, yeah?"

Ryan shrugs. He whacks the ball between the two coats we're using for goals.

"Less of that too!" says Wheeler. He runs after the ball and blasts it in the air.

Ryan and I chase after it.

Bonus Bits!

Guess Who?

Match the fact to the person from the story. Check your answers at the end of this section (no peeking!).

A works at Quickstop

B spotted by a talent scout

c played for United in the 1970s

D plays in the under-16 team with Jackson

E supports Arsenal

1 Taylor

2 Jackson

3 Arthur Logan

4 Mum

5 Ollie

Quiz Time

Can you answer these questions about the story? Look back to check if you need to. The answers are at the end of the book.

1. Who said, "Who is that old geezer watching us?"

  A Taylor

  B Wheeler

  C Harj

  D Jackson

2. What did Ollie keep secret from Jackson to begin with?

  A that he is friends with Ryan

  B that he lives next door to him

  C that his dad is the manager

  D that he plays on the youth team

3. Where is United's Academy and training ground?

    A Samuels Park

    B Winter Hill

    C Jacksons Park

    D Spring Hills

4. Who used Jackson's phone to post the comment that Liam was angry about?

    A Jackson

    B Ryan

    C Wheeler

    D Ollie

5. What position does Javier Souza play at United?

    A right wing

    B goalkeeper

    C centre half

    D central midfield

6. What position does Jackson most like playing?

    A right wing

    B goalkeeper

    C centre half

    D central midfield

7. Which character used to drive taxis?

    A Granddad

    B Arthur Logan

    C Alex Chambers

    D Liam

8. What does Jackson see in the hallway of Ollie's house?

    A an old-fashioned telephone

    B a tall coat rack

    C a huge fish tank

    D a miniature football pitch

WHAT NEXT?

If you enjoyed reading this story, why not look for other football stories?

Think carefully about what Jackson had to learn during the story. Can you think about what he needed to be good at and focus on in order to be a good footballer?

Why not make a poster that could be displayed to attract young footballers to the game? Try to include all of the qualities they would need to be successful.

ANSWERS to GUESS WHO
A7, B2, C5, D9, E1

ANSWERS to QUIZ TIME
1B, 2C, 3A, 4B, 5D, 6D, 7A, 8C

Look out for more of Jackson's adventures!

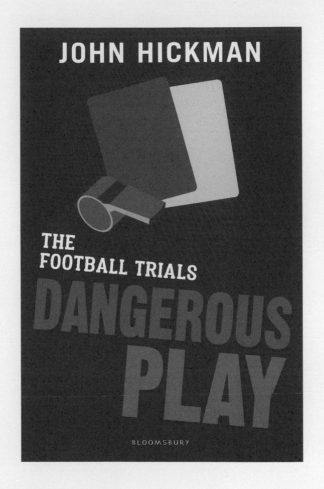

JOHN HICKMAN

THE
FOOTBALL TRIALS

DANGEROUS
PLAY

BLOOMSBURY

978-1-4729-4415-3